PENGUIN MODERN C

The Memoir of an Anti-Hero

Kornel Filipowicz (1913–1990) was a Polish novelist, poet and screen-writer. He studied biology in Krakow and lived in that city for most of his life. His first book of poetry, an edition of ten copies, came out in 1943 and established him as a leading figure in the Polish avant-garde. During the war he was arrested and imprisoned in the Gross-Rosen and Sachsenhausen concentration camps. In later years he became a close friend of the poet and Nobel Laureate Wislawa Szymborska, with whom he exchanged thousands of letters. The first of these he sent in April 1966, enclosing photographs of monkeys from Krakow Zoo.

Anna Zaranko is a translator from the Polish, Russian and French. She lives in Jesmond Vale.

KORNEL FILIPOWICZ

The Memoir of an Anti-Hero

Translated by Anna Zaranko

PENGUIN BOOKS

PENGUIN CLASSICS

UK | USA | Canada | Ireland | Australia
India | New Zealand | South Africa

Penguin Books is part of the Penguin Random House group of companies whose
addresses can be found at global.penguinrandomhouse.com

First published in Polish under the title *Pamiętnik Antybohatera* by Czytelnik 1961
This translation first published in Penguin Classics 2019
This edition published 2020
001

Copyright © the Estate of Kornel Filipowicz, 1961
Translation copyright © Anna Zaranko, 2019

The moral right of the translator has been asserted

Set in 11/13.7 pt by Sabon
Printed and bound in Great Britain by Clays Ltd, Elcograf S.p.A.

A CIP catalogue record for this book is available from the British Library

ISBN: 978-0-241-35160-4

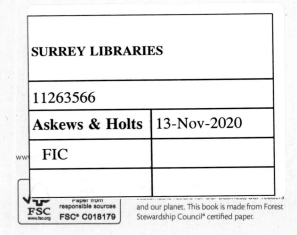

Although human life is priceless, we always act as though something had an even greater price than life . . . but what is that something?

Antoine de Saint-Exupéry

"The outbreak of war found me in X, a beautiful place in the foothills where I had spent my holidays the last three years in a row.

By the end of August, almost all the summer holiday-makers had packed their bags and left on the crowded and now late-running trains. I'd been to the station twice and I'd seen the goings-on. I told myself that what the majority did was not necessarily what one ought to do – and I stayed.

So, on 5 or 6 September (I had a room in the garret of a wooden house with a little balcony, near the road), after an hour's gunfire – which, on the advice of the landlord, I'd spent in the cellar – I saw the Germans. Their equipment, discipline, briskness, bearing – they were astonishing; this was something more than a victorious army. The Poles, whom I was seeing now as prisoners – were something less than vanquished; they were destroyed. Annihilated. I want to be frank in what I write, and I have to say they did not stir even my pity. I don't consider myself completely incapable of that sentiment. But they were simply . . . disgusting. Disgusting, threadbare, dirty and brutish. Animals in rags. A slightly risky comparison, but nothing better comes to mind. I'd been in the army once, but I had no idea that the same uniform – boots, weapons and kit – could so easily lose their look and meaning.

The day after the Germans invaded, there was an incident in one of the neighbouring villages, not yet occupied at that point: a local teacher (I saw her soon after and I'll describe her in just a moment) hid in the attic of her school and waited there several hours for the Germans to arrive; she knew they were approaching from the Secretary of the District Council who had a telephone. So there she was, waiting in the attic and looking out of the window with a machine gun by her side. It was, as people recounted later, an RKM Browning, recently introduced into the Polish army – light, with twenty-five-round magazines. She had maybe three or four of these magazines. There was a small meadow not far from the school with volleyball posts; she used to take her pupils there to exercise. The teacher watched as the Germans drove back and forth along the main road, bypassing the school from a distance. All around was quiet; no echoes of war. It was not until evening that a few cars and motorcycles arrived on the meadow. The soldiers got down from their motorbikes and left their cars, smoked cigarettes, had a bite to eat. There was even the sound of a radio playing from one car. The teacher slowly pushed the end of the barrel through the small opening of the little attic window and began to fire. She fired and fired, using up every single magazine. And to think she fired a hundred cartridges and killed only two Germans! I saw her the next day; they were taking her away in an open car. She had on a black polka-dot dress, her mouth was twisted, a dark patch under her nose, one eye closed as though she were still taking aim, matted hair – a proper drowned rat. Madwoman. Is that how a hero is supposed to look? To hell with such heroism! It was repulsive! There was a German officer on either side of her. One wore gold-rimmed spectacles. Both had very calm, human faces.

I spent another two weeks in X since I considered a return to Z inadvisable at that point for a number of reasons. The weather was beautiful. I took walks in the direction of the bridge. I'd buy a newspaper on passing the station kiosk and circle around along the river by way of return. I'd sit down on a tree stump by the riverbank where only recently I'd been coming to bathe, and read the newspaper. It was, to begin with, the same paper I used to take before the war; a little later, it changed its name. Part of the editorial team had taken on the job, explaining that they were doing so to continue serving society, reporting events and directives from the new authorities. Then, alongside military communiqués, political news and official announcements, notes began to appear on breeding rabbits or protecting trees for the winter, jokes and anecdotes, even the philatelists' corner was revived. It was a pathetic substitute for a once substantial paper, yet proof at the same time that certain fixtures remain in our lives, though people and authorities may change. Even though the war continued, the railways were working, the postal service functioned and the village headman was at his desk – bah! Yesterday, I even saw a funeral procession leaving the church. The most ordinary of funerals, a country funeral for some peasant who had died of old age.

I'd sit on the bank at a spot that I liked, read the newspaper and think. (It was a calm and relatively shallow bend in the river, with nothing impeding a clear view of the riverbed.) I thought: armies fight armies, overcome and rout them – and the country remains the country. The war is still going on – but the outcome's already determined. Why does the war still go on? The news reaching

us daily left us in no doubt. Three days after Bydgoszcz
and Kraków – Radom and Łódź fell. Within the next
three days, the Germans had surrounded Warsaw and
reached Lwów. A few pockets remained, tightly encircled
by German divisions; the surrender of the Polish troops
squeezed in there was only a matter of time. The exact
day depended on the amount of ammunition those units
had at their disposal. Not a chance.

The town of X was empty and peaceful. The Germans
stayed two days, then packed up and headed east. There
was no gunfire to be heard; all was still. When I sat by
the river in the afternoons, I often heard the hum of aero-
planes above; they flew very high, skirting our parts.
Towards evening, they'd return south.

One night – it was just before my departure from X – I
was woken by a loud knocking at the door. For a moment
I didn't answer, I pretended to be sleeping; I listened out
and thought. The landlord was away; he'd gone to get
planks from the sawmill at N, intending to stay the night,
since there was a curfew. The sixteen-year-old son of the
house was off at scout camp when war broke out and they
had no idea where he was right then. I listened intently:
there were no voices or scuffles to be heard outside the
door, but the knocking was suddenly repeated.

'Who's there?' I asked.

'It's me,' I heard the voice of my landlady. 'Please sir,
could you open the door?'

'What's happened?'

'I'll tell you, sir.'

I put on my trousers and slippers and opened the door.
The landlady was right in the doorway. She stood clutch-
ing a shawl to her chest. She said in a whisper, 'My son
has returned from the war . . .'

'Well, that's good.'

'Yes, but please sir, could you come down with me for a minute . . .'

We went downstairs to their flat. A strong light bulb shone harshly. The window was curtained with a blanket. A sixteen-year-old boy lay on the bed, sleeping; his mouth was open and he was snoring and moving his tongue as though about to say something. His face was sunburnt and dirty, with a bruise on his forehead and picked and festering pimples around his lips. He wore an old-fashioned cloth uniform, probably dragged out from the very bottom of a heap at some mobilization depot. The uniform's sleeves were rolled up, but still too long. It looked as though both the boy's hands had been cut off.

'Poor old thing, asleep before he'd even stretched out properly,' whispered the landlady.

'So let him sleep.'

'But, sir, I don't know what to do!'

'Nothing. Change his clothes for civilian ones.'

'But, sir,' she touched my elbow and indicated the wardrobe. In the corner beyond the wardrobe, and perfectly visible, stood a rifle, leaning against the wall. It was a long, heavy Mannlicher from the First World War, withdrawn from active service an age ago. That kind of weapon was used only for military training now.

'Maybe it's loaded?' asked the landlady and looked at me. There was no fear in her eyes, only curiosity and a kind of malevolent bestial gleam.

I released the lock; there was no ammunition in the barrel. The chamber and magazine were empty too. I closed the lock, dropped the trigger, and put the rifle back in the corner.

'But what do you think, sir? What should I do?'

'What should you do? Get the hell rid of that useless

bit of iron!' I said. I would willingly have left right then in order to have nothing more to do with it.

'Get rid of it? But where? Ah, if only my husband were here!' said the landlady, looking at the rifle.

'How do I know? Chuck it into the woods, or the water somewhere,' I said, but then I realized that the river's bed was visible even at its deepest point. 'Throw it into the cesspit and *basta*,' I said, losing patience.

'The cesspit?' the woman stared at me, and again I saw that savage flash in her eye, quite distinct this time – hostile and determined. 'The cesspit?' she repeated. She straightened her scarf and moved decisively towards the dresser. She opened a little door, took out an electric torch and handed it to me. Then she took off her scarf and spread it out on the table. I stood there like an idiot with the torch in my hand and watched what the woman was doing: she lifted the rifle clumsily with both hands and placed it carefully on the table, then began to wrap it painstakingly in the scarf. I glanced at the boy: he slept, moving his lips. He must have been very tired to sleep in that bright light.

I asked, 'What are you doing?'

'We'll hide the rifle. You can light the way for me, sir,' she said. She picked up the gun and pushed at the door with her foot.

We went outside. The night was cold and dark. I tried the torch.

'Quiet! Not yet, please.'

The woman paused in the middle of the yard and listened. Somewhere far off, a dog was barking. Otherwise, it was as peaceful as though nothing had happened in this country. The woman moved off in the direction of the woodshed. She opened the door and said, 'Now, sir – switch it on.'

She shoved aside some rusty hoop, metal sheets and planks. Underneath was a heap of decaying, blackened sawdust. The woman dug out a hole, slid in the rifle and covered it over. She placed a sheet of metal and some bean poles on top. I stood and watched her quick movements, like a small animal scrabbling in the ground with its paws.

Then I returned to my room and looked at my watch: it was four o'clock. I didn't go back to sleep; I just packed my things and made the bed. Then I sat, smoking cigarettes and thinking. The war was ending; something new was beginning. It was nonsense to sit and wait for it here, among the crude and stupid. In times like these, it was hard to know what to expect of such people. One could easily get mixed up in some idiotic pickle without even realizing – no matter whose side it was on. The incident with the rifle was warning enough.

When it got light, I washed, ate breakfast, bade my landlady goodbye and headed for the station. I left on the first train that came.

I found my flat in Z in perfect order. A few letters had piled up in the mailbox. Two belated postcards, a month old, from holiday pals hoping we might meet again some time. A friend from Zakopane, curious where I was, expressed concern as to my fate. Her letter was dated the day before the outbreak of war. For the rest – some government lottery brochures with their clover emblem and optimistic slogans, and a slightly testily composed reminder concerning payment for the furniture and carpet taken on instalments at Grunberg's. However things worked out, I could be sure that Grunberg would not be so insistent in future. In the cab coming from the station, I'd seen a few Jews wearing six-pointed stars painted on armbands. It meant that Jews were now subject to some sort of special regulations; it was, of course, a dubious honour. I had many Jewish acquaintances, I was even on quite intimate terms with some of them – but ultimately their fate was a source of indifference to me.

The room was stuffy, so I opened the window. To my satisfaction, everything was in its place. War had swept the country, but despite it I'd survived and found myself among my things again; here was the divan with its little *hutsul* kilim, the club armchair in the corner, not a leather one, of course, but very comfortable and modern. Next, the elegant, glazed bookcase with its walnut veneer. A few books inside which I liked to keep at hand: the 'Great Geography' and 'History' volumes of Gutenberg's Encyclopaedia, dictionaries, statistical yearbooks. Then my little round table, two little chairs. A plush Żywiec carpet on the floor. Reproductions by Stryjeńska on the walls. A little bureau by the window and a lamp with a rose-tinted shade. A shiny new bicycle leaned against the wall. Four months ago, a certain extremely eloquent salesman, no doubt working on commission, had almost forced me to sign a purchase agreement for a bicycle. I would be its rightful owner after twelve payments, that is, in June 1940. And now I'd actually become its owner significantly sooner. It was a similar business with almost all my possessions; even the books were only half paid for. I was amused when I realized: it was my private victory in this war. There was still the gas and electricity to check – they were on. I knew about it from the press; now I had proof that it was true about the Stadthauptmann signing off the declaration activating the electric power plant and city gas supply. I put on some water to make tea and set about unpacking my suitcase.

That afternoon, I went into town. Military gendarmes with shields pinned to their chests were standing at the crossroads, directing traffic. A megaphone had been set up on one of the squares and communiqués were being announced in Polish. The high command of the German armed forces was informing us that Marshal Rydz-Śmigły had fled to Rumania and that the battle of Kutno had ended in the complete liquidation of two Polish armies. With this news, I went to the café where, over a cup of now ersatz coffee and some tiny cakes, I met a few acquaintances. Some of them were wearing officers' boots and military breeches and made no effort to hide that until a few days ago they had been German prisoners. The fact that they were allowed to escape was supposed to show that the Germans were stupid. I learnt what people were thinking and saying: everyone agreed the war would last at least a year. It would take that long, in their opinion, for the tardy West to switch from peace- to war-time production, mobilize its reserves and go on the offensive. There was no doubt as to the outcome. France, together with Belgium, Holland and the English auxiliary corps, commanded enough strength to detain the Germans at the Rhine for as long as it would take to bring over American assistance and organize landings in Italy, the Balkans and Scandinavia. A German defeat was only a matter of time. Two forces would settle the Germans' fate: strikes by Allied landing troops from the outside – and uprisings inside the occupied territories, in Poland, Austria, Czechoslovakia, blasting the empire apart from within. One older, retired officer whom I knew from the bridge club, said, 'And in the meantime – on alert.' He had in mind the state to be observed by all of us citizens able to carry arms. Someone remarked that, after all, we Poles had some practice in conspiracy – you might call it hereditary.

Such were the conversations conducted around café tables where, at the same time, trade burgeoned in dollars and gold, and a little later, in anything you might dream of. The transactions were cashless – only quantities and timescales were discussed and addresses exchanged; the seller was to pay a fixed commission. I didn't get involved; I was convinced that the Germans wouldn't tolerate a black market for long. Besides, the people behaved provocatively towards the Germans: they whispered, turned their heads nervously, sniggered and nudged each other. It was the disgusting behaviour of the weak, the conquered. I stopped frequenting the café.

Warsaw fell presently, and Hel surrendered a few days later; General Kleeberg's units capitulated, having spent all their ammunition. The lists of the dead, prisoners and military equipment reported daily in the paper grew to new proportions. The war was over. A little later, the geographical term 'Poland' was annulled and the Germans introduced a new concept in its place: the *General-gouvernement*. I marked the borders of this territory in which I now found myself living with a red crayon on the map in my 'Great Universal Atlas'. As I drew, I thought about the impermanence and transience of states. This conclusion came not entirely without regrets; I was, after all, somewhat attached, or perhaps accustomed, which comes to the same thing, to the name and dimensions of the state in which I'd lived until now.

The weather was beautiful. Autumn slowly approached. The days were sunny, warm, and clear as glass. Only the nights grew gradually colder. One morning, I decided to make use of my new bicycle and visit an old school friend who had a small market garden eight kilometres from town. I'd run into him on the street one day; he thumped me on the back and said we should be helping each other now, and since I had a bike I might visit him from time to time. We could have a bite to eat, a drink, talk politics and

I could bring back a few kilos of potatoes and something to go with them – keep the old stomach from grumbling. I pumped up my tyres, donned a light casual suit and my sunglasses, and set off along the clean asphalt which was slightly damp after the night. The bicycle went like clockwork. I rode along slowly; at the crossroads, a blue policeman, only recently in charge here, waved a command for me to stop for a column of tanks to pass. They were returning from the east, decked with flowers, pine branches and trophies: Polish helmets, gas masks and cavalry lances, their ragged banners fluttering. One tank bore a whole collection of insignia: 'Biłgoraj District Authority', 'Helena Strychacz – midwife', 'Zamość Air Defence League'. The soldiers were tanned and well nourished; the ones sporting the shields smiled as we looked on. Then came the anti-tank units covered in tarpaulins and, finally, officers in jeeps brought up the rear. The synthetic petrol smelt sweet in the fresh morning air.

The column passed, the policeman made a half turn and indicated with his white-gloved hand that the way was clear. I leaned on the pedal and pushed off. I turned left along the convent wall, and then along a narrow street leading towards the market square. At the end of the street, at its exit, the sun, obscured by the buildings, slanted its light low from the side, making people and objects appear as though in an aquarium, in some strange substance which bent the light differently. I had known this town from childhood and, truth to tell, if I was attached to anything, it was perhaps only to the walls, the air and the trees which flourished splendidly in our town. The buildings on the left threw deep, cold shadows across the asphalt. I passed a caretaker sweeping the pavement, then a nun in a great white cornet walking beside the wall, taking tiny steps as though she were moving along on invisible little wheels. I was fast approaching the square, just at the street's exit – when suddenly . . .

I heard the squeal of brakes, clutched at my own, stopped and looked straight into the windscreen of a military vehicle. The doors on both sides opened, two SS-men got out. One stopped, the other approached with a quick step and slapped my face across the right side and the left.

He yelled, '*Ach, du polnischer Trottel!*'

I fell onto the pavement along with my bike. I heard the double slamming of the doors and the car drove off. It happened so fast that it all seemed to take place simultaneously. Lifting the handlebars, I noticed that my fingertips were grazed; the blood quickly began to flow. I took out my handkerchief and bound my fingers. Someone said, 'Son of a bitch . . .'

The nun, her cheeks red, said quietly, 'You've hurt yourself, sir. You must go to the chemist on the corner and get some iodine.'

I felt disgust and hatred for these people and their sympathy. I would have been happy to see them meet exactly the same fate on the next street corner. I looked down at my trousers and saw a triangular tear on my knee through which I could see the skin, scraped to bleeding. I took a safety pin from under my lapel and pinned together the torn material. Then I stood my bike up, got on and set off home. I rode slowly, careful now, and cautious. My hands and legs trembled slightly, my muscles felt stiff, but I controlled myself. The policeman at the crossroads indicated that the way was clear. As I passed him, it seemed to me that he was gazing intently at my face. I realized that I no longer had my sunglasses. To hell with them.

Back home, I washed and doused my wounds with iodine. I changed into pyjamas and lay down on the divan. I lit a cigarette to calm my nerves and then I began to think. Above all, I asked myself: what should be done to secure my personal safety and safeguard my belongings? That is, to live and remain in this room, among my books and things? Apart from what was left of three months' salary, I had no savings. What use would they be, in any case, even had they been in paper zlotys. This money of ours, which had seemed so robust and solid, and even just recently had been so difficult to acquire – was losing its value from day to day and would soon be no more than scraps of paper. Money had met the same fate as the army, the government and the people who had so recently been someone and meant something. Should I buy gold and dollars with what was left and use that? I had too little capital to live on the interest that exchange transactions could supply. In any case, it was a risky business; I was convinced that the Germans would not let it continue for long. Or maybe I should follow up what acquaintances were doing: I'd heard of people working in some brickyard or in quarries; one person, I was told, had gone to work on the trams, another had joined the railways; some university lecturer was a waiter, a former mayor was selling cigarettes in a kiosk. I have a Masters in economics, I'd had a good job of late in industry, and I was a correspondent for a certain paper in the capital. I had been someone – was I now to be no one? Maybe run away abroad, as yet others had done? The escape itself was now too great a risk, and then all the rest – all that complete unknown. How long was the war going to last? An acquaintance once said in the café that he would rather feign dumbness for the entire war and pound rocks at the roadside than utter a single word in German. Fine prattling. In a month or two, when he feels the pinch, he'll start hunting for work and cease to have scruples. There are no heroes. But then, what do I know, maybe

there are; in any case, I'm not qualified for heroism. The
army which was supposed to defend my country and me
has lost the war. The country has been occupied by the
victors. I belong on the side of the losers and I have to
succumb to those who now rule the country. No doubt
there'll be lunatics who still want to resist. Most of them
will perish and their heroism will perish with them.
Those few 'heroes' who manage to survive the war – their
heroism will soon be forgotten. Such will be their fate.
Throughout history it was ever thus. But let's pause just
a moment: let's suppose that it matters to me that history
should not forget me. To qualify for the title 'hero' – I
would have to perform some completely exceptional act.
(Overlooking the fact that I'd always associated the notion
of 'heroism' with someone not quite right in the head.) On
top of that, I'd need a heap of luck to ensure my deed was
recorded for posterity. About as much chance of that as
winning the lottery. Let's suppose I got lucky. One basic
obstacle remains: I feel absolutely no desire to risk death
merely to attain posthumous glory . . .

I became quite cheerful; I shifted on the divan to reach
for a cigarette and felt a sudden sharp burning pain in my
knee. The rotten thing was going to end up festering. I got
up, made a cold compress and lay down again. I lit a cigarette and looked out of the window through which I could
see the building opposite. An old lady sat on the balcony,
her knees wrapped in a blanket, and looked through the
railings down into the street. Sometimes she'd turn her
head and glance into the depths of the dark, empty flat.
I'd been watching the old lady on the balcony for years; on
warm clement days, they'd put her out in the sun. In the
winter, the old lady would vanish. Each spring, I'd be convinced that she'd died, but then the old lady would appear
again, just the same – frail, withered, indestructible.

No doubt, the majority of people in this country want the Germans to lose the war. But there's no certainty that the Germans will lose. There is not a person who can give any guarantee regarding that or, indeed, my own future. No one has the right to demand heroism of me; no one has the right to demand that I remain a tram conductor to the end of my days, a caretaker, or a freight company guard – a nothing. My life, my health is my greatest good – *basta*. No one has the right to question that. I want to live; I want to live well and be someone. I want to be sure that I won't be persecuted, reviled, treated as a lower category being. I have no sense of solidarity with persecuted creatures; they disgust me!

*

Was it rotten of me? Perhaps, but it was certainly astute. No one can deny that. Two years have passed, those two years that my café acquaintances meant to survive by trading and gossiping or, as that friend of mine threatened, pounding rocks by the roadside. And here's how Europe looks today: France is defeated and humiliated; the Germans have occupied Denmark, Norway, Yugoslavia and Greece. French, Belgian and Czech steelworks are producing guns and tanks. The whole of Europe is working for the German army, which is moving east, crushing the opposition of the Soviet forces. I no longer frequent the café, but at work I encounter people who, in these two years, have lost none of their truly Polish optimism which is, in any case, characteristic of a primitive mind. These incurable optimists feed on illusions: some minor complication, a momentary halt in the offensive (the adversary is still resisting, after all), a brief setback in Africa, an unclear situation in Russia – all are supposed to signal the beginning of the end. They listen to the radio, pass leaflets around, compose rhymes and consult the cards. England has never lost a war! America is preparing slowly, but systematically! Meanwhile, Russia is drawing the German armies into its icy depths in order to devour them, as it did the Napoleonic forces in 1812! This is the kind of thing I hear around me. And the young conspire, mess with firearms, play the partisan. These youths are impudent and stupid. They parade around town in long boots – then, beaten up, ragged and dirty, they wend their way to German concentration camps or to the clay pits beyond town. Those remaining free play the hero still. They recently dragged three of them out of the building opposite, where the old lady lives – two young boys and a girl. I hadn't seen the old lady for a fortnight and I thought she'd died. But today – a beautiful, sunny, almost warm November day – I saw her again, sitting out in her wicker chair. I have to say, I greeted her with joy: Good morning, old lady! You know what life is worth. You know that best of all – every day – there's your stool, your helping of groats, a cup of tea, a grated apple. It's worth living just for this!

*

There was an unpleasant incident at the beginning of winter, but I have to congratulate myself that I came out of it with the upper hand, and even benefited considerably, since I consolidated my position in our building. It was like this: I'd had a few guests over the night before – a couple of Germans and two amiable ladies. We listened to records, had a few drinks – not many. I tend to avoid this kind of gathering, but I had to do it just the once; it was necessary, given my position at the office. Early next morning, when I was leaving for work, I got smacked on the back with a snowball. It was so unexpected a blow that for a second I thought I'd been shot with a revolver. But then I heard shrill childish voices: '*Volksdeutsch!* ... *Volksdeutsch!* ...'

A second snowball shot past me and stuck to the wall. A horribly cold stream of water ran down my neck and spread under my shirt. I went out onto the street and without looking back took ten paces forward. Then I spun round suddenly – but I saw no one. I turned into a neighbouring gateway and lit a cigarette in the passage. When I looked out cautiously a moment later, I saw my persecutors: the caretaker's children, just as I'd suspected. They were leaning their heads out of our building's gateway, but they were looking in the opposite direction.

A few days later, at the casino, I made sure to run into a certain German whom I knew worked at the Kriminalpolizei and asked him for a particular favour. I explained how I envisaged it.

He heard me out and then slapped me on the back: 'Sooner or later, that cunning Polish nature always emerges with you people. All right then. But what do I get out of it?'

'Two kilos of sausage and a bottle of Baczewski original.'

'You be careful, you *Schwarzhandler*!' he cautioned me, wagging his finger. 'All right; it's a deal.'

I endured some lingering uncertainties after the caretaker's arrest. The arrest itself was quick and efficient. During the search, they found a kilo of illegal veal which the caretaker peddled, like all caretakers in any case; they also confiscated *The Knights of the Cross* and some other Polish books. The first part of my plan had gone perfectly. Now came the second, much harder, part.

Two days later, leaving for work in the morning, I called in at the caretaker's place. The children hid under their quilt when they saw me and the caretaker's wife burst into tears.

'Excuse me, but is it true that your husband has been arrested?'

'Jesus Mary! But why? Why?'

I sat down and said, 'Well, it doesn't take much to be arrested these days. Someone bore him a grudge, informed on him and there it is. You know what these times are. It's not the point. I've come to try and help you.'

'Mother of God, if only it were possible, then my husband . . .'

'Please, calm down and listen: I can't do much. I don't have any contacts there. But I'll try to find some-one . . .'

This, more or less, is how my conversation with the caretaker's wife began. I did it with disgust, straining for sincerity all the while. The woman cried almost the whole way through. She was a very ugly, small, meagre woman with a veiny neck and thin hair. I didn't look at her throughout the exchange. I attempted to smile at the children who were lying in a horrid, dirty mess of bed-ding. Above them hung a framed oval picture of Christ and his apostles, walking through a wheat field. Corn-flowers bloomed among the wheat and larks were visible in the clear sky. I repeated that I would do whatever pos-sible, but I couldn't promise a result.

I endured a few more days full of uncertainty. Those were very hard moments for me. I feared the German would do the dirty on me; I feared for myself, for everything. Then at last, one evening, I heard my doorbell ring and there stood the caretaker. He was shaven and combed and smiling. He placed two bottles of vodka on the table and unwrapped a paper package of ham, goose and some other meats.

'What's this, Mr Rubiś?'

'It's for you . . .'

'Oh no, Mr Rubiś. Please, take it all away . . .'

'But it must have cost you.'

'Indeed, it did cost me, but not money, only health and humiliation, doing the rounds and pleading. I did it simply for you. I don't have any contacts "there" and so it wasn't easy. I did it just for you, and for your wife and children. Do you understand?' I said, my tone quite rude. The caretaker was disconcerted; he didn't know what to say. 'Well, let's have one glass, to drink to our success,' I said kindly after a moment, as though I were feeling sorry for him.

The caretaker filled the glasses eagerly; we downed a shot each and chatted for a moment. I said I had an urgent job on: an article to translate from German to Polish on the planting of hops, and I despatched my victim out of the door together with the goose, vodka and smoked meats. Once he'd left, I breathed a sigh of relief. I lay down and lit a cigarette. The action I'd undertaken to protect my peace and security had been nerve-racking, but I had to do it. Children are stupid and come up with nothing of their own accord. I could just imagine what was being said about me in the building! Now I'd shown myself a saviour, a good man and, more importantly, a disinterested one. The chattering would cease. Now I could pass for a slightly mysterious person at most, maybe even someone who worked for some organization? No matter. It was a game well played. And I'd learnt something new about myself in the process: I wasn't a half-bad actor. It might come in handy some time.

*

So once again my life grew peaceful, following its now ordinary course. I devoted only vague attention to my relations with the Germans, since I'd ascertained the wisdom of not permitting myself to be drawn too far into intimacy with them. Their military position in Europe and in Africa had begun to deteriorate a little lately. No, deteriorate would be putting it too strongly; let's say it began to get a little complicated. Naturally, the optimists were readily triumphant; I contented myself with scepticism. In the end, it's possible that the new partners in this great game, Russia and the United States, might prove to be stronger than the Germans and better organized.

I had an amusing encounter recently. A few days ago, at dinner in the Stadtkasino where I sometimes go, a soldier in an SS uniform paused by my table.

He clicked his heels and asked loudly, 'May I?'

'Of course, do sit down.'

'Thank you,' the SS-man replied. He turned, removed his belt and coat and hung them up. My German is passable – and in any case I've made some effort in the course of the last three years to acquire a good accent – but the soldier evidently detected something in my speech since he asked, 'Are you, by any chance, from Memel-Gebiet? I have the impression that we've met somewhere before?'

'No, I'm a German from Wołyń,' I answered, as I'd have little to say on matters Baltic. I was finishing my soup and wasn't able to observe closely the person with whom I was conversing. Besides, my eyesight is not the best. Thanks to this small flaw, I was dismissed from the army with a category 'C', and was able to avoid taking part in the September fracas. I wiped my mouth with my napkin, raised my eyes – and it was then I saw his eyes. It was the same SS-man who had slapped my face three years ago.

'Ah, I was about to say. Beautiful part of the country, isn't it?' he said, seating himself opposite me.

'Beautiful, but savage, barbaric,' I replied.

'Oh, you're right. I've just returned from those parts. We have some difficulties there, a mass of difficulties,' he said in a quite melancholy tone. He picked up the menu and studied it at length and in detail. I don't know what he expected to find there, since the menu listed only four items: soup, a second course, tea and beer. 'But we will organize this country, believe you me. We will pacify it and bring it to order. One day, it will be a land flowing with milk and honey!' he added with animation.

This man did not recognize me. I observed him while he was eating his soup, and I was waiting for my second course. I noted his nose, slightly reddened from frost, his narrow lips which parted to take the soup, revealing long white teeth with several gold fillings. Clean and shaven, the man's fresh uniform smelt of the warehouse and slightly old-fashioned eau de cologne. I felt no hatred towards this man. I felt nothing; I was completely indifferent. Although, actually, I ought to be grateful to him. He had essentially made me what I am; he had pressed upon me the stamp of citizenship, which allowed me to get through three years in peace. He knew nothing of this. But he also had no idea that, were the Germans to lose the war one day, I would be disgusted by them. I would despise them and hate them.

I left the clean, fragrant soldier to his tankard of beer and went outside. The weather was slightly misty. A huge orange sun was descending in the west. A bitter frost was taking hold.

*

The previous year had been a hard one for me; it dragged on intolerably, every day brought annoying incidents. Not that I still had hopes of the Germans winning the war; I'd long ceased to count on that. Some might retort that not so very long ago, I'd counted on just such a victory. First – that was three years ago. Secondly – I didn't want the Germans to win; I simply took it into consideration realistically. Did I express it differently three years ago? Perhaps. I don't deny it. A person changes. Well, the Germans succumbed to the will of the adversary. That was a year ago, and I'd been in little doubt since as to how the war would end. But the world is hell-bent on all possible means of complicating and delaying the ending of what has already been determined. I suffered not as a result of the losses sustained by the Germans, or indeed all participants in this war, but through their stupidity. The story, once again, of all wars that drag on beyond their time, if I can put it that way, beyond the time in which they should have been settled. Some might think that for me, personally, it would be better if the war lasted considerably longer. Not true, there could not be a more stupid assumption. I wasn't so great a coward as that; I was not a complete coward. (I don't think I am a coward at all – the concept is completely alien to my character.) In my situation, the quicker defeat comes, the quicker I can put what must follow behind me. But how the Germans dragged on, how horrendously they dragged it out.

One day – it was the beginning of September 1943 – I arrived at the office in the morning to find none of the Germans there. It was most unusual. A moment later, I discovered that all the Germans were gathered in the director's office and, from beyond the doors upholstered in brown oilcloth, their outraged voices could be heard.

There were two Poles working in our office – a porter and a messenger – but they, too, were absent. The messenger had gone to the post office, and the porter, as always at this hour, was standing in a queue with food cards to pick up our rations. I had no radio, though I had permission, and I was completely unaware of what was happening. It was intolerable. The conference in the director's office stretched on; I sat at my desk and began flicking through papers, thinking as I did so of how it would be if, tonight, say at 2.20, it transpired that the Germans were to sue for peace and gunfire were to cease on all fronts at that moment, and after a few hours the representatives of the warring sides were to sit down together to discuss the terms of capitulation. It wouldn't be the worst moment to choose: best done when one's own armies are still engaged on foreign soil. For me, personally, it would be most advantageous. In the barbaric confusion which accompanies battles and the shifting of fronts, in the savage atmosphere of revenge, retaliation and individual reckonings – in such circumstances, my fragile and delicate human existence would be a hundred times more vulnerable. Unfortunately, it was not yet the end of the war; I learnt this presently when my office colleague, forty-year-old Miss Riemendorf, a specialist in carbon-copy bookkeeping from Koblenz, returned to the room in which I was working.

'Good morning, Miss Riemendorf,' I said. 'I apologize for my two-minute lateness, but it's bucketing down.'

'Good morning, good morning. You have strong nerves,' replied Miss Riemendorf. She sat down at her desk and began opening and closing all the drawers in turn. I looked at her: she was even uglier than usual. I had always suspected her of drinking. Today, her little face was even more than usually grey and lined.

'Why, what's happened?' I didn't have to pretend; I really was alarmed.

'Don't you know?'

'I have no idea, Miss Riemendorf!'

'The Italians have capitulated!' said Miss Riemendorf very loudly and looked at me as though I bore some responsibility for what had happened.

I felt embarrassed; I didn't know what to say. I was silent for a long moment, and then, trying to make my voice sound as natural as possible – I wanted my reply to indicate that I was seriously concerned, but not in a panic – I asked, 'How exactly did that come about?'

'The Führer has been expecting this for some time. They are very much mistaken if they were counting on surprising the Führer. Now, when things are not going quite so well for us, it becomes evident what our friends are worth. But the Führer will not be disappointed in us Germans. You'll see before long what will happen!' said Miss Riemendorf; she looked at me and pursed her narrow lips. Then she slammed her drawer shut, as though she'd re-cocked a rifle.

I held her look, nodded my head, and said, 'Yes, yes . . .'

The following day, the newspapers reported that the German armies were hurriedly manning the Apennine front and disarming the Italians. A few days later, a certain exceptionally audacious German parachutist freed Mussolini from prison and flew him to Hitler's quarters. I saw them both in a photograph: Hitler was severe, tense, his hand caught motioning in mid-air; Mussolini in civilian clothing, a shapeless hat on his head, stood opposite, helpless and exhausted, hands hanging idle at his sides. His proud face was dark now, sunken, expressionless and pointless, like the face of someone mentally disturbed. The SS-man who had rescued him from prison stood to one side, with a sly, disdainful smile. He was natural and savage as a cat. He was the only real figure of the three – even though this savage killer (who bore a very expressive Slavic name besides) seemed ready to spring up at any moment and disappear into thin air. Those two were unreal, though each in a different way. The person in a crumpled hat was no longer a dictator – he had lost what had been most vital in him – his role; Hitler was still a leader – but for how long? That he would cease to be so was certain now and deprived his figure of force and meaning. I imagined that he himself, Hitler, must now be feeling very insecure in his role. I gazed at his frozen gesture in the photograph and it suddenly seemed to me that, in order to make it, Hitler must have overcome some terrible inner constraint, fear and uncertainty. The one undoubtedly self-assured being of the three in the photograph – whose role was indisputable, clear and distinct – was the SS-man. This Slavic warlord in the service of the Germans had neatly and flawlessly – 'einwandfrei', as the Germans say – executed a task of no use now to anyone. It was our style. I even felt a certain liking for him.

But I've gone too far. My imagination ran away with me. I wanted quickly to put behind me what had to come. Where was it supposed to be coming from? From the West, or from the East? For me, it would be a real salvation if it were to come from the West. But what difference could I make? All I could do was wait.

Indeed, waiting equated to living I repeated to myself daily, in order not to lose a sense of the value of what I'd preserved to that point – but my life was contracting from day to day.

I left the house at half past seven and walked to the

office to avoid using the tram; in the German section, pretty empty as a rule, I would be exposed to nasty glances from the Poles, crammed tight beyond the cord; if I were to travel in the Polish section, I would risk harassment from the Germans, and an eventual meeting with the director or Miss Riemendorf. My personal situation was ambiguous enough already. The Germans simply took me for a Pole, the Poles for a German, whereas I was neither. I had brought no harm to either one or the other; my whole fault lay simply in the desire to save my skin in this rotten business. And so I went on foot, changing my route frequently for reasons I will outline shortly. Work hours were meant to last until four, but I rarely managed to leave at that time. I was among those who, if the need arose, were ready to stay at the office until evening. Officially, my zeal was surely recognized and often commended – I was held up as an example – but I grasped in time that one shouldn't overdo it. I had already heard more than once from Miss Riemendorf: did I intend to sleep at my desk today? This with bitter, poorly disguised derision in her voice. I was close to crossing that line beyond which I, a non-German at the end of the day, was not permitted to go; but luckily I realized in time. So I would leave the office late in the afternoon, buying this or that to eat on the way, and return home. I stopped going to the Stadtkasino for dinner; I attended no parties – other than the absolutely necessary. I stopped going to concerts, the cinema or theatre.

This routine had been prompted by something of which I've not yet spoken. I must tell it now in more detail. I once tried to recall when it had all started, but the beginnings are elusive. I overcame the first slight anxieties and doubts quite easily with the help, so to speak, of auto-persuasion: come on, man – what are you afraid of? You're not Gestapo or a Nazi dignitary. You've hurt no one. Go on, take a look and check, there's no one at the door; look around, no one's following you. Stand at the curtain and look down into the street: that man's no combatant from some underground organization with a pistol in his pocket; he's just a boy waiting for a girl with whom he's off to the park, that's all. At first, I managed quite well, but more and more often my inner dialogue failed to take effect. I felt safe only in the office and partly, not completely, at home, behind closed doors, locked and double-latched. I had only to step over the threshold to be immediately assailed afresh by fears and delusions: suspicious-looking people were standing in doorways, signalling my presence to each other with their eyes, then someone would tread behind me, staring obstinately at my torso. One day, I was close to stopping, turning suddenly and shouting at the top of my voice: 'What do you want from me?! Why are you persecuting me?! Leave me alone!' I don't know how far I really was from beginning to shout – it seemed like a close thing to me.

Tales of the cruelties perpetrated by underground organizations were disseminated with particular enthusiasm in our office by Miss Riemendorf; in Miss Riemendorf's version of events, the underground's chief victims were *Volksdeutsche* and Poles. I don't know how much truth there was in these stories or to what extent they were born of Miss Riemendorf's feverish imagination, but one of them proved to be true: it concerned a certain Pole whom I'd known before the war and who'd been working at the Arbeitsamt. One day, he was shot through the door of his flat. Miss Riemendorf, who knew the layout of my flat, described the event as though it had taken place in my home. I don't know if she did this deliberately to provoke me – but it was from my door that the splinters flew, and my body that the bullets pierced (Miss Riemendorf tapped at my chest with her sharp finger), and travelled on, through bathroom and sitting room, shattering basin, mirror, vase of flowers and windowpanes along the way.

In any case, the times grew increasingly horrible: Germany was still pursuing war, and still had great, almost unbroken armies. Impenetrable and well-armed fronts stretched across the whole of Europe – but the Germans had completely lost control over what occurred in places where a German soldier happened not to be positioned at any given moment; he merely had to turn away for a second, and behind his back cunning individuals would immediately begin to sabotage, torch and murder. The whole country was turning into one great conspiratorial camp of partisans. I'd often find leaflets and news-sheets in my postbox now. They were produced by various organizations – beginning with imperialists and ending with communists – but you'd learn essentially the same thing from all of them: the days of Nazi Germany were numbered. There was also information concerning concentration camps, executions, notices of sentences carried out, and, lately, very business-like articles discussing future political and economic questions. At first, I'd read these scraps of paper, but then I stopped. I'd throw them into the stove, tip on some paraffin, set them alight and wait for them to burn and carbonize. But still they'd leave fragile, black and crumbling remains, smouldering here and there, retaining the form of crumpled pages, even traces of letters. I took particular care that nothing of the sort should be left in the fire; I beat the remains to dust with a stick. I suspected that my supplier, if not of all, then certainly some of this literature, was the caretaker, the one I'd saved from prison, and perhaps from death.

(Had I not, in fact, saved him?) Whenever he bumped into me, he'd always pull knowing faces – and I would respond discreetly: I'd wink, then rub my eyelid, as though I had an itch. Sometimes, we'd exchange a few perfunctory remarks on the subject of the frost, the heatwaves, rain or drought.

Presently, other afflictions tagged on to my psychic obsessions: an upset stomach, I began to sleep badly, I was irritable – I, who had to be so much in control of myself – my memory began to falter. One day, I finally went to the doctor, first to a German, and then, not trusting what I'd heard from him, to a Polish doctor with a practice at the other end of town. For obvious reasons, I did not confide the subject of my anxieties to either one or the other; I spoke generally of nervous exhaustion, sleeplessness. I complained of impaired memory and stomach ailments. Both, as though in collusion, prescribed similar sleeping draughts and tranquillizers and told me more or less the same: that all these were the symptoms of one great illness from which we were all suffering, and the symptoms of this disease would subside as soon as the war ended. Meanwhile, they advised a vacation, a great deal of fresh air, bathing and walks – and both were of the opinion that women were a first-rate remedy for my sufferings.

The women in my life! There'd been some of course – more rarely of late. I'd been panic-stricken with fear of venereal disease since my youth and avoided casual encounters. This was the result of schoolboy perusal of literature stimulating the imagination and the deterrent example of university friends of whom so very few had the luck to avoid the consequences of love pursued in municipal parks. During my studies, I'd conducted a romance with my landlady, a childless widow sixteen years my senior, with whom I lived for three years. It conveniently combined the question of lodgings with what my friends had to pay for and often rue. I lived with this woman as with a wife for three years, but it left me with a revulsion for marriage. That ageing little widow allowed herself too many liberties: she'd come into my room at any time of day or night, she'd dart about the flat half-dressed, often she'd sit down to table in her nightdress, she'd call me 'my snot-nosed little hubby', or simply 'my child'; she wanted to bathe and dress me. Towards the end of our acquaintance, she herself had ceased to wash; she had evidently assumed that we were too seasoned a married couple to mind such trivialities. In the third year of my studies, I left her; I simply didn't return to the house after the holidays. I had a few more problems with her later: she'd pester me, write letters, threaten to kill herself. Which she never did. I'd see her sometimes in the street; she had exaggeratedly rouged cheeks, wore some pitifully pretentious hats (I remember she used to make over the hats herself) and, dressed in very short skirts, she'd be rushing somewhere, weighed down with bags and boxes.

During my first position in some horrible, borderland county town, I had a fling with a quite pretty intelligent little thing, the wife of the deputy mayor. She was a spirited woman, very temperamental, two or three years older than me. Her husband, who must have been a quarter of a century older than her, a quiet man with a friendly smile, would take solitary evening strolls by the river, his hands clasped behind his back. Meanwhile, his quick-witted wife would drop in at my bachelor rooms and begin to undress hurriedly as soon as I'd closed the door behind her, hurling insults at me all the while as a scoundrel and ruffian. This dragged on for two years, and then, when I moved, we saw each other until the war broke out – on holiday or at my house where she would stop off for a day or two on her way to see relatives.

In that same provincial town – where one spent dull afternoons flirting, playing cards or drinking vodka – I had a strange adventure, with considerable cost to my health at the time. Krystyna, the wife of the deputy mayor, had a friend, Zofia, whose husband taught drawing and gymnastics at the local grammar school and was a cavalryman in the army. One evening, the most unexpected thing in the world: the wife of this cavalryman knocked at the door to my flat, apologized for visiting a man who lived alone, sat down at the table without removing her hat with its then fashionable veil, and requested a moment's conversation. She reminded me that, as I probably knew, she was a close friend of Krystyna's and I should not be surprised by what I was about to hear. My romance with Krystyna was an open secret. It was left only for Krystyna's husband to learn of it, who, like all husbands, would be the last to know of his wife's faithlessness, but sooner or later, know of it he would, since that is the way of things in this world. I was completely disoriented. The woman from whom I was hearing this was sitting opposite me and looking straight into my eyes. She was very pretty, young, with that borderland Ukrainian beauty: a pale, serene face, black hair, dark eyes, a thin delicate nose, straight as a ruler. She looked at me – and I did not know what to do with this prize. Her husband, a stout drunkard, inveterate gambler and brawler, an uhlan in the army, had a horrible, red mug; some said he was a lecher who couldn't let a single woman pass – others jeered and mocked his brawn, claiming they had good reason to doubt his masculine prowess. One way or another, he was a frightful person; I saw him sometimes at the military club where he'd get up from the card table in the early hours, unshaven as a gypsy with the bloodshot eyes of a knackered horse. I didn't know what to do; I asked her to grant me a moment to take it all in and fortify myself with a glass of wine. I took out a bottle of wine and two glasses, and poured one for each of us. She didn't refuse. She drank half a glass, but our conversation was heavy going, I mumbled inanely – finally, I don't know how it came about, I embraced her. She sat motionless, as though turned to stone, her face sombre and her forehead furrowed. When I pulled her towards the divan, she began to resist vigorously, but I couldn't stop myself by then; I felt that would be the worst. I slept with that beautiful, strange, taciturn woman that evening, despite so fearing her husband. I have to say, I'd have given a lot to have had her many more times – but it didn't come to that. She didn't come again – and I was simply frightened. I often caught sight of her at the casino, silently accompanying her horrible card-playing husband – red, unkempt, stinking of sweat like a horse. She never looked at me. I left that awful town three years before the war. In 1939, Zofia's husband found himself abroad, where he carried on serving in some Polish military formation.

I found that out from her two years ago, when I bumped into her in the street. She also told me that she was passing through and that she lived in the country, in the Lublin province. I proposed she stay with me then, said I lived alone, but was told she had a very important meeting in half an hour and was leaving that evening; perhaps she would drop in some time. She left me her address and asked me to write. I wrote, but waited some two months for a reply. She informed me in a postcard that she'd changed address and was planning to visit me some time. A few more months went by, until one evening, just before curfew, she appeared at my place – and stayed.

She remained two days: taciturn as before and somehow generally reluctant. Seeing her too elegant for wartime lingerie, I joked that she must be trading in gold and dollars. She replied curtly, 'Something like that.' Then, after a moment, she added that she was now called Zinaida Hominiuk, 'What, you've changed your first name too?' I asked, thinking that she'd remarried. 'Yes, I've changed my name and surname,' she replied and no more was said on the subject.

These were the only two women I saw during the occupation: Krystyna more frequently; Zofia twice in all. Krystyna's old and now completely decrepit husband had died at the beginning of the Occupation. Zofia, too, was apparently a free woman, so to speak; her husband was on the other side of the front, and one does not return so easily from today's war. There were moments when I thought: how would it be if I were to bind myself to one of these women in a permanent way, even to marry one of them? I surely wouldn't be the worst of matches for them. But how great is the distance from a thought to an action. I never dared be the first to propose it. To be honest, I didn't know what made these women tick; for me, they were slightly incomprehensible beings. I was pleased when they arrived, and when they left – I greeted my regained solitude with relief, a return to old habits, to peace and independence.

Both these women, so different in temperament, were very much in accord on one point: that it was very astute of me 'not to meddle in politics'. Krystyna once told me, lying by my side at night when the sirens were wailing – that it was good to know that nothing threatened me, that I could be visited again and found well and whole in the same, safe place. But I didn't believe them; I told both one and the other at some point that I suspected them of saying one thing while feeling another. That they preferred a man to be a risk-taker, as long as providence preserved him from the consequences of his recklessness. I heard from both one and the other that I did not understand women. But I still didn't believe them.

*

The summer of 1944 was bright and hot. I'd already embarked on a health regime, as recommended by my doctors, back in the spring. I modified their advice a little, adapting it to my situation and capabilities. In my circumstances, it wasn't possible to organize the convalescent leave both doctors had prescribed. After all, I couldn't go off to the countryside with my documents. It was very difficult to get a place at a sanatorium because of the horrendous number of wounded filling the health resorts which were allocated to the Germans. Instead, I bought a Swedish exercise manual in a second-hand bookshop. The purchase alone lifted my mood. It was a little book written forty years ago in a contrived style and embellished with appropriate illustrations: the author-cum-instructor posed for the photographs in a striped knee-length costume and bore an incredible resemblance to Hitler. The same little moustache, the same hairstyle, the tight tense face, similar posture. The little book bore the title *My System*, and comprised an historical introduction and ten illustrated lessons which, diligently executed, were meant to ensure health, success and longevity. It closed with excerpts from grateful letters to the author, including from a certain Mecklenburg pastor who wrote that, thanks to the manual, he had regained inner peace, family happiness and the respect of his flock . . .

    It's odd – I was aware, of course, of the humorous

aspects of this health handbook, yet I diligently carried out the exercises devised by the author who, in his fore-word, announced further publications: *Return to Nature* and *Towards the Sun*. Every day at six in the morning, beside a wide-open window, I did squats, inhalations, exhalations and bends in the frosty March air; I thrust out my arms, rolled my head and jogged around the table, my fists clutched to my chest, just as my ridiculous teacher recommended. I took great care that no one should see me at these exercises; I kept well away from the window. Opposite, the only flat on a level with my windows was that of the old lady, who might anyway have died, for I hadn't seen her in a long time. After exercising, I would go to the bathroom, shave, wash and dress. I then had greater occasion than before to examine myself – my body, muscles and skin. I'd never been overly taken with my own person, but now, perhaps thanks to that amusing double, or rather precursor of Hitler from half a century ago, I'd found occasion to take an interest in my own physicality, and as a consequence I had a new occupation: I began to pay more attention to my somewhat thinning hair, the state of my teeth, nails, calluses, pimples; but that's nei-ther here nor there. The fact is, I regained a considerable part of that sense of well-being that I'd previously enjoyed. And how very much I needed it now – when the Russians had long since crossed the Polish border and when the ultimate defeat of the Germans was only a matter of time. I had survived the worst; the great change I feared still lay ahead – but let it come as quickly as possible, since it was inevitable; let it all be over. If I wanted to go on living – I could not avoid it.

I didn't take a summer holiday that year either. This time, proof of unfading zeal on my part was received with pleasure by my German colleagues in the office, and particularly by Miss Riemendorf, whom I promised to replace, and who no longer troubled to hide her disgust for Poland, having hopes that, after the holiday, she would not be obliged to return to this, as she now termed it, 'eastern European' country.

So I didn't take a holiday, but, if it was fine, spent every free afternoon and every day off by the river on the outskirts of town. Its banks and bordering flat and treeless meadows swarmed with crowds. By the riverside – among the swimmers and sunbathers lazing on the grass, dressed only in a bathing suit – I looked like everyone else. There was nothing labelling my body to say who I was. I undressed, rubbed cream into my skin, lay down on a rug spread on the ground and – read, thought or simply dozed. The sun moved across a clear sky, the scent of water spray hung in the air, there were sounds of laughter, the shouts of children, and the hoarse cries of ice-cream vendors, pushing their shabby carts ahead of them, full of ghastly muck smelling of nail polish. When I was bored with dozing, I opened my eyes, looked about, then returned to my reading: *Rome of the Caesars* or *Genghis Khan*. Occasionally I got up, did a few squats, bends and jumps as recommended by Dr Picius, the author of *My System*, or I cooled down by plunging into the river's murky water which reached as far as my stomach. Sometimes, when the swarming and buzzing around me grew too intense, I'd up camp. I'd take my clothes, rug and book under my arm – and move ten paces away. Once, when a group of fifteen-year-old brats were lounging around nearby, reciting 'Ordon's Redoubt' and 'To a Polish Mother' by heart and far too loudly at that, I gathered up my gear and forded the river along the stones, settling down again in peace on the other side.

The weeks went by, the Russians pressed forward

relentlessly. The Germans were still holding the front, but had lost their grip on life within the country. The German administration still held sway over the bigger towns – but in the provinces, the villages and woods, the partisans roved impudently. I waited and grew calmer all the time. It was a state very like that in which I'd lived through the first days of the war. The fate of the Germans was a source of indifference to me.

But I must be cursed with bad luck. Always, at the most unexpected moment, something revolting happens. One day – it was a peaceful, still and slightly misty Sunday morning – I set off for the river as usual. I was one of the first trippers. It was still chilly; in the shade, a cold dew lay on the grass. I did a few exercises, then immersed myself in the clean water, still undisturbed by bathers. Around ten, it began to get hot and the banks began to swarm with people. I made myself a little sun-roof with my shirt and a stick, sipped tea from a flask and, amid the yells of children, barking dogs, whistles, the sounds of a ball being kicked, the patter of feet and wild leaps into the water, I dozed off.

I started suddenly and, half-conscious, heard cries of, 'Run, gendarmes!' Shots resounded somewhere, very close by. At first, I wasn't at all clear what to do; I think my initial, half-conscious reaction was to run away and I even took two or three steps towards the river. But I don't remember; it all happened like a dream. The Germans were approaching from the meadows; they advanced in a half-bow, fanned out. On the other riverbank, along the side to which I'd wanted to flee – gendarmes and blue police loomed up as though from beneath the ground. I was now completely calm, or, to put it better, perhaps – indifferent. I dressed without haste. The Germans were coming nearer and surrounded us, letting only women

and children through. Again the crack of a rifle shot; some
boy had sprung up suddenly like a fleeing creature. I saw
him, how he fell and lay there, his leg twitching. The
Germans passed by, ignoring him completely. I was as
perfectly calm as the time I took double pain relief for
toothache. I sat down on the grass, wiped my feet, put on
my shoes and socks. When the gendarmes were close, I
got up and waited, my face turned towards them. A tall
German with a protruding nose and close-set eyes was
approaching in my direction and looking at me.

I said to him in German: 'I'm a German.'

'Identity papers!' said the German quickly, quietly.

It was at that moment I realized that I didn't have my
papers with me; that I had not a single scrap, even in
Polish, confirming my identity, that I'd left all my documents at home. I began, like every idiot at such a moment,
to pat my pockets, looking for what I did not have on me.

'Well?'

What's worse, my strength deserted me at the same
time. Something odd happened to my jaw, as if I were
seized with cramp. I began to mutter rubbish in broken
German, as though I barely knew the language. I felt a
slap across the face and heard a voice in a language which
I understood perfectly.

'We've already got one without papers. Hold onto him,
so he doesn't scarper!'

The gendarmes continued, leaving groups of men
behind them under the guard of the blue police. Some
people attempted to find out what awaited us from the
policemen, but they were taciturn; one said our documents
would be checked and then we'd be released. I glanced at
my watch: it was just past twelve. A tremendous heat was
building up. The boy whom they'd shot as he was fleeing had stopped moving his leg. He lay motionless in the

grass, flies crawling over his shoulders. I thought it could be that brat who'd recited 'Ordon's Redoubt' so loudly. I asked the blue policeman if it was all right to sit down. The policeman didn't answer, he shrugged and turned away. I sat down on the grass and lit a cigarette.

Some fat fellow bronzed by the sun in a patched check shirt asked me for a light. When he'd lit up, instead of thanking me, he said, 'Why did you say you're a German, idiot? Fat lot of good that'll do you . . .'

Little white clouds appeared in the sky from the south, but they all obstinately shirked the sun and gave no shade.

There was no inspection of documents. The gendarmes had completed the round-up, now they stood in groups, talking amongst themselves and smoking. They seemed to be waiting for something. It soon transpired what: along the lane a column of trucks appeared, skirting the meadows; they approached slowly in our direction, raising a flurry of dust behind them. They came to a halt near us. A moment later, I found myself along with others in the prison courtyard. We were lined up facing the wall, ordered to put everything we had on us on the ground and raise our arms, and then we were of no further interest.

We were surrounded on three sides by a high wall topped with barbed wire, the prison building with its iron-grated windows behind us. It stank intolerably of Lysol, lavatories and rotting potatoes. The sun beating down became increasingly unbearable, the walls were thumping out heat like bakers' ovens. I stood with my arms raised and thought: how long can we bear this? That was the only thought crossing my mind now and for some time to come. I could see someone's back in front of me, the shoulder blades shifting fitfully under his shirt. Some of those standing swayed as though about to fall at any moment. It was perfectly quiet, someone passed behind me, their shoes crunching on the gravel. Someone whispered something; someone else was panting or praying; someone began to cough. The sun was burning my forehead. I hung my head and looked at the ground; it was strewn with fine cinders and crushed brick. A huge puddle of urine had collected at the shoes of the person in front of me. I lifted my head, closed my eyes, leaned my head against my arm. I felt my raised arms growing numb, and they began to ache and hurt. I inclined my head towards the other arm, which brought a moment's relief. People began to behave a little more freely – they fidgeted, whispered, shifted position, some lowered their hands and rested them clasped on their heads. I decided to do the same; the physical bliss that I experienced for a moment was intoxicating, but all too brief. I must have decided too late to defy their discipline, or else it was my usual bad luck – as a fierce shout pierced the air:

'*Hände hoch! Maul halten!*'

I raised my hands; the others did the same. Again a hush. I'd gained a moment's respite, but now felt my situation all the more keenly. I began to think: what am I actually waiting for? After all, I've nothing in common with the people surrounding me. I've ended up here by accident. If I don't protest immediately, then every extra second of delay will further legitimate my presence here. If I don't make a protest, it means that I consider the first, chief and universal crime weighing upon all those around to be equally applicable to me: that they're Poles. Regardless of other offences that many of them might have committed. Now, instantly, I should lower my hands, turn, approach one of those behind me and say calmly: '*Es ist ein Irrtum . . .*' – yes, that's a splendid phrase. There's been a mistake. I'm a German, and as a German, I demand an immediate explanation of this misunderstanding. So my thoughts went, but why didn't I act? Again the minutes and quarter-hours went by, I stood as if tethered. Even though I felt my arms growing weary and my legs growing numb – I was incapable of moving from the spot. Then suddenly something happened – as though what bound me fell away, as though all my brakes were released: I turned, dropped my arms and began to walk towards the entrance of the prison building where two SS-men were sitting on a bench.

One of them, the younger, leapt up from the bench, reached for his pistol and shouted, '*Halt! Halt!*'

I stopped and said, 'Hear me out, please. There has been a misunderstanding, I'm a German. I demand an explanation for this misunderstanding and to be released.'

I said this calmly and smoothly. My spoken German was again flawless; my words were perfectly intelligible to them. I felt that now all was well, that German law had begun to function in my regard.

The young SS-man put his pistol back in its holster and the older one looked at me. He asked, 'How come you're here?'

'I went to the beach in old clothes I seldom wear. I simply forgot to take my documents.'

I was led to the prison office, my details were taken down, also the name and home number of the director at the office where I worked. The NCO dialled the number and got through to the director's house, but he wasn't there; the NCO was evidently told that he would return later, as I heard him give the number of the prison and say that when the director returned, he was to telephone immediately. I was taken to an empty cell and locked in.

I sat on a stool by the window through which nothing could be seen. I had no particular thoughts; besides, it's not important what I thought about. I was calm, I waited.

From time to time I glanced at my watch. Around six
o'clock, I heard voices behind the door, then the key scraping in the lock. My director was standing in the prison
office: his red face had caught the sun, his eyes were
round and startled. A party pin shone in the lapel of his
blue jacket. He looked at me, but said nothing. The two
SS-men were in the office and a Gestapo officer, his uniform unbuttoned at the neck. The Gestapo man said, 'So
this gentleman claims to be a German, employed in the
office where you are director? Is this true?'

'But of course!' my director replied very loudly, almost
shouting.

'Well, it's fortunate you're a German,' the Gestapo
officer said and sat down at the desk.

I was released. Walking across the courtyard, I saw
people were still standing there, hands raised just as they
had been six hours ago. An elderly man was lying on the
ground, his eyes closed, breathing fast. With every breath,
his whole body trembled like a jelly. Next to him, his
peaked cap lay on the gravel, and an old leather case, a
flask of milk stopped with paper peeking out of it. I don't
know why, but I saw all this very precisely, as though it
were a photograph. My director didn't look at anything;
he coughed and wiped his nose on a handkerchief. When
they let us out of the prison gates, I said, 'Thank you,
sir . . .'

My director didn't answer. He continued to wipe his
nose, sniffing and wheezing. After a long pause, having
restored his nose to order, he stowed the handkerchief
in his pocket and said, 'May I just say: you are an idiot.'

We went on in silence. I felt happy. It was a warm,
fragrant evening. The sun had set already, dusk was
falling, but the sky was still bright. The swifts swooped
and whistled between the tenement walls.

*

I sat in my flat and waited for the moment when the shots would fall silent. I told myself one had to sit it out, like a storm, like something there was no way to avoid. It seems to me that everyone would do the same in such a situation. But was the place I'd chosen the best of shelters for such a moment? I had given it a great deal of thought lately. There's no need to run over what passed through my mind; in the end, it's what I did that counts. There were a hundred ways to weather the moment – I chose the most straightforward.

And so I sat in my flat. The door to the corridor was solidly locked, the curtains were drawn. I had some supplies in my larder – tins, sugar, dried food. I could last even a month, if it came to it. My office had ceased to exist about a week ago. All the Germans, including Miss Riemendorf – her face intolerably contorted recently – had left. I too had received an evacuation order, but had made sure on the day to be neither at the congregation point nor at home. I spent half the day in quite a curious place: at the allotment summerhouse belonging to our caretaker. It was hardly a suitable place to spend the night just then. I sat in that summerhouse, snow-banked on all sides, on a narrow stone-cold bench in the frost. I smoked and looked through the window, thick with cobwebs, and listened to the sound of change drawing in from the east: the still distant, but unbroken thunder of artillery and the rumble of high-flying planes. Through the window, you could see levelled plots, broken fences, beanpoles. Crows were flying west in the grey sky. They flew in whole flocks, then singly, a few together, and flocks again. At dusk I returned home, chilled to the bone.

I spent the next two days lying on the divan in my

room. I heard the storm approaching, gathering strength, ceasing and diminishing, and again approaching. I waited for it to reach the town, and scoop up the street and house where I was living. A hundred thousand Soviet soldiers were working non-stop, day and night, in snow and frost, to force back a hundred thousand German soldiers. The front was coming closer – but so slowly! Other than terror, only one emotion still accompanied me throughout the hours of waiting: the desire that what must happen should happen as quickly as possible. I remember when I was fourteen years old, I experienced the death of my grandmother in the same way. She was a long time dying, all day and all night, and I sat in the loft, on a crate of flour, and waited for my grandmother to die; I think I might even have prayed for it to happen at last. I wasn't present at my parents' death; they spared me that sight. They died in my absence.

The sound of the artillery grew closer with every hour. I lay and waited for the missiles to start landing on the town and on my house. But I never got to see that day. Towards evening, the guns subsided, and I fell asleep in my clothes. I woke up frozen, with a heavy head, aching with the throng of tormented dreams. There was ringing in my ears; it was cold in the room. The town lay peaceful, with only an occasional rifle shot somewhere far in the distance. Could it all be over? I stood by the window and parted the blinds: no, it was not yet the end. German wagons dragged through the streets drawn by peasants' horses. The peasants were doing the driving. In the carts sat Germans; some had their heads bound in dirty bandages. All were ragged as beggars, dirty, unshaven; faces pale as corpses. Their rifles were stacked any old how, as though they had no further need of them. It was a disgusting sight. I dropped the blind.

There was neither electricity nor gas. I'd used up the last of the coal yesterday; I would have to go down to the cellar for more. Right then, I wouldn't do that at any price. I got undressed, climbed under the quilt and, to avoid losing any body heat, I covered myself with two blankets and a coat. I wound my watch and placed it next to me on a stool. The quiet rattling of wheels reached me from the street, sometimes a motorbike or car drove past. The sounds of individual rifle shots could be heard in the distance; they rang out as if those shooting were doing so reluctantly, or had nothing to shoot at. How it dragged on! And why? Why did this war which the Germans had already lost go on? The worst moment for me was approaching, the transition from one state to another. Would this change be preceded by some 'interim', in which the town would be nobody's? So long as it didn't last too long. I didn't feel good; I was nauseous, maybe from hunger, or cold, or simply out of fear. What's more, I didn't feel like sleeping. I felt the loud beating of my heart; thoughts crowded my mind without rhyme or reason. I lay there, yawning, my skin itched; sleep did not come. The time dragged by, there was no way of hastening it. At some point, I told myself that I really had to do something, to occupy myself somehow, or I'd go mad. I got up, lit a candle and looked at my watch – half past one in the morning. The room was gripped by a cold so bitter that every movement caused physical pain. I opened the larder and took out a bottle of vodka, surprised at myself for not thinking of it much sooner. It was foul, standard issue, pure vodka. I opened the bottle and drank a glass of the nasty stuff. The taste of that liquid was dreadful; I never could stomach pure vodka. But after a few minutes, the alcohol began to take effect: it warmed me from the inside, braced my jittery body and returned some sense of

well-being. I swallowed a few more glasses, then I took
one of the sleeping draughts that the doctor had once prescribed. It must have been the biggest drunken spree of
my life.

I went back to bed, covered myself with every possible
thing and thought over various matters for a long time;
for example, I imagined that the Germans had returned
and Miss Riemendorf was sitting at her desk opposite me.
I have to admit, it was not the most pleasant of thoughts
that could have occurred to me. I switched subjects and
began to recall Zofia's last visit, then a vacation by the
sea – and I fell asleep I don't know when, unexpectedly,
as though I'd suddenly fallen over a precipice.

I woke with a terrible headache, with a stiff, as though
paralysed neck. It was frightfully cold in the room; from
behind the porous curtains, the bright glare of day pene-
trated from outside. I looked at my watch: it was two in
the afternoon. I dressed and stood listening for a moment:
it was quiet in town. No shots to be heard, nor the sound
of engines. Only what seemed to be the thunder of artillery somewhere in the distance. I raised the blind at the
window, but the panes turned out to be frozen from top
to bottom. I didn't want to open the window, so I armed
myself with a knife and set about scraping clean a section of pane. I cleared the white, crumbling ice, rubbed
the pane with a handkerchief and looked out: I had only
a section of the street in view, together with the gateway
opposite, the windows of the first floor, the pavement and
a strip of road. The first people I saw along that patch
were two boys. They were pulling along a sled loaded
with crates and tins. The boys were very preoccupied,
they gesticulated as they talked; clouds of steam rose from
their mouths. They disappeared quickly and for a long
moment there was no one to be seen – then . . . Here

I must pause, because I'm not sure I can convey what I felt at that moment. Nothing comes to mind; if I were to say that I was horrified, it would be equally false as true. I could just as well say that I felt relief, or experienced great joy. I'll simply describe what I saw: so, I saw two Soviet soldiers. They were young men, approaching with a swinging gait: one was dressed in black leather overalls, the other wore a padded jacket. Both were armed with small short automatic rifles which they wore slung across their shoulders, barrels pointing down. The soldiers vanished. I worried away at the frozen shutters. When at last I managed to open the window, I choked on the icy air. I peered into the street: there were people walking along the pavement carrying bread under their arms, struggling with bags and backpacks laden with something. I leaned out and at the corner of the street I saw a great tank with a five-point star. It stood motionless, one track propped on the pavement. Three soldiers were eating soup from a steaming cauldron. People stood about, watching them. A light breeze lifted and tossed some coloured papers about the road. I closed the window. So it had happened. The one clear and certain thought that came into my head then was the wish that whatever had happened should now be irreversible. Now, when what I'd feared most had come to pass and I was alive – it was necessary to try and preserve my existence; I felt a flow of energy and resourcefulness.

I ascertained with satisfaction that the electricity was working. I could put on some tea. There was no gas or water, but I had some water reserved in the bathroom. I had to wash and shave. The first thing to be done was to fetch coal from the cellar and light the stove. That was the place to begin.

I put on boots, I wrapped up in a fur coat and I went out into the stairwell with my coal bucket. I hadn't seen

my dirty wooden stairs for three days, yet it seemed to
me a very long time since I'd been there – as though I'd
returned from a distant journey. Loud conversations
could be heard beyond neighbours' doors. I quickened
my step; I had no intention of hiding, but at that moment I
preferred not to be seen; I was dirty and unshaven. Downstairs, I found terrible ruination: something had happened
while I was sleeping, in the night or towards morning. The
entrance gate had been blasted off its hinges, the stained
glass adorning the external door was shattered and the
floor was strewn with coloured shards. In the corner, I
saw a pile of cans from German gas masks and helmets;
cardboard boxes, rags, papers, photographs. Water from
somewhere, probably a cracked pipe, had streamed over
the ground creating a slide along the corridor, flowed
down the cellar steps and frozen into icy cascades. I
thought that war should not relieve the caretaker of the
duty of sprinkling something so slippery with ash. I des-
cended sideways, step by step, holding onto the wall and
lighting my way with a candle. Finally, I found myself
safely downstairs; my coal cubby was in a dark corner at
the end of a blind corridor. I reached into my pocket for
the key to the padlock and then lifted the candle high.
That's when I saw him.

He was lying on his side, face to the ground, legs bent
at the knees. You could see the studded soles of his shoes
and one hand turned palm upwards. The soldier wore
no belt; there was no rifle lying nearby, nor any other
weapon. He'd been wounded and was looking for a shelter
in which to die; and he'd chosen just the spot right at the
foot of my cellar door! The door opened outwards and to
get to the coal, the corpse would have to be moved. I was
all alone with this now dead body – but was it really dead?
I prodded it with the tip of my shoe. The body in the green

coat was still and hard as stone. I tried to move it with my foot: it wouldn't budge. I kicked it once, twice, a third time. This dead German's lifeless mockery was irritating. I kicked him again and again, in the legs and shoulders. My mouth repeated some curses – you swine, you bastard, you just had to crawl in here to kick the bucket, you shit . . . I came to my senses only when the candle went out and hot stearin scalded my fingers.

I managed to light a candle a moment later – I say managed, but my hands were trembling as though I had a fever and I couldn't find the matches that I'd only just used. To move the body, I had to touch it with my hands. There was no way around it. I forced myself somehow, but it turned out that I was in no fit state to do it; my muscles were powerless, incapable of anything, as in an anxious dream. I put the candle on the ground, and using both hands, braced myself with all my strength and, overcoming what seemed to me the resistance of some incredibly heavy and inert mass, I eventually shifted the corpse away from the door. I opened the padlock and entered my cellar where I had three tons of coal. It rose right to the ceiling in a great glistening heap. I leaned against the wall, breathing laboriously in the heavy, stale air. I felt the sticky sweat sliding off my forehead, my heart was beating so hard beneath my clothes that I could feel its rhythm in my throat, arms and stomach.

I was deadly tired after my battle with the German corpse.

*

I was ill for several days. My arms and legs ached, I felt nauseous and done in. It's possible I had the flu or even pneumonia. My temperature soon dropped, but I was left weakened. I lingered in bed, a scarf wound around my throat, though my throat wasn't sore. I fooled myself that I was ill, with a kind of internal approbation that I evidently needed in order to maintain psychological equilibrium. I didn't shave for days, I avoided physical exertion, I neglected all but the most essential activities. But there's no absolute control over the workings of the brain. The brain, and one of its powers in particular, the imagination, is able to live a life independent of our will. Not to speak of dreams. The dreams I had! But that's beside the point.

This state of mine was actually just a waiting for the final act. My windowpanes thawed. Now I could watch what was going on outside. But I lived quite far from the centre of town and along a side street, so I couldn't see all that was happening on the main roads. I didn't see the army march through. I witnessed neither gatherings nor rallies. Only once did I see a column of marching German prisoners escorted by Polish soldiers. An abomination. I remember that once, at the beginning, when writing about Polish soldiers going into captivity in September 1939, I opined that the Poles were something less than a conquered side, that they were undeserving even of mercy because they'd been annihilated and seemed disgusting to me. And how did the Germans look now? They were dirty, shabby, with no belts, without emblems or insignia. Their uniforms which had once seemed so cleverly considered, easy and stylish, now hung from them like senseless rags. They trudged along slowly, some were limping, one trailed a grubby scrap that had attached itself to his boot. Their faces? They had no faces. Black, empty holes gaped between their collars and caps. It was as though they were walking not into captivity – but into nothingness. I turned away from the window.

I sat in my room, lived off bread and tinned food, and waited. Not once did it occur to me to run away. I didn't flaunt myself particularly, I didn't wander the streets needlessly – but everyone knew of my presence in the house; my neighbours were aware of my existence, the caretaker knew, the local shopkeepers and the kiosk man. But even so, I waited almost two weeks for those in charge of these things to take an interest. If they only knew how I waited for that moment!

At last, one morning – I was actually shaving in the bathroom at the time – I heard a short ring of the doorbell. Two young people were standing in the corridor, one in an army uniform, a pistol at his belt, the other in civilian clothing. The one in uniform asked my surname, after which, on hearing me confirm it, both of them entered with a step as confident as though they were old acquaintances of mine. The civilian said quickly, 'Get dressed, citizen, you're coming with us.'

Instead of the usual words probably said at such moments, 'What's going on?' or 'I'm sorry, there must be some misunderstanding', I asked:

'May I finish shaving?'

'Shave then, shave,' said the civilian and glanced at the one in uniform. I returned to the bathroom and picked up the razor I'd placed to one side. The uniformed one followed me, stood in the doorway and watched as I shaved. I could see the interior of my room in the mirror. The civilian stopped by the bookcase and looked at the books, twisting his head to see the titles. They were mainly Polish; I had very few German books. The civilian circled the room, opened and closed the cupboard doors, lifted the throw on the divan, picked up *Rome of the Caesars* which was lying on the table and leafed through it. I was completely calm. I finished shaving; my hand functioned without trembling. Smooth, clean skin emerged from under the blade. They had permitted me to shave. 'Shave then, shave,' they'd said. They were granting me a favour. I disgust them, but they rise to an act of mercy. What ordinary, weak, stupid people. It would have been unthinkable for the Germans. I had a kind of foretaste of the times to come: the judgements would be harsh, but certainly not so consistent. Was that worse for me, or better? Not a clue. Probably worse. I would rather not have to count on the unpredictable in a person.

At last I was calm and sure of myself; the place I was headed was my goal and could not be avoided. I had to pass through it. At the same time, it was the safest place under the sun for me. I felt the terror had slipped away, that terror which had held me in its grip all the years of the occupation. I felt lighter and lighter, healthier, free of all the ailments that had beset my fearful body.

'What are you so cheerful about?' asked the civilian, who, after his stroll around my room, was back at the bathroom door, observing my face closely in the mirror.

'I'm happy the war has ended,' I said. And it was true.

The civilian looked at me as though I were a lunatic. After a moment, having concluded I was not, he said in a threatening tone, 'It hasn't ended for everybody . . . Get a move on, dress!'

I had no intention of bantering with these barbaric young victors. What a charming example of the primitive that civilian was; how unsure of his role the uniformed functionary. They had no idea whom they were dealing with. I took my time dressing. But I was a little troubled by something – as though I had a tooth-pulling ahead or some small operation to which I had to submit in order to carry on living in peace.

*

At first, I was in a small cell in the company of an old gentleman who rarely addressed me; he would spend whole days pacing up and down. I attempted, unsuccessfully, to strike up a conversation with him. He replied to the point, but briefly; he never confided anything, nor did he question me. He gave the impression of a person who'd risked great adventures in life. During my stay in the cell, he was taken twice for long interrogations. He came back grave, silent and concentrated. Then he would promenade up and down the cell again, pondering something. He was someone; you could feel it. I wouldn't have been surprised if, on leaving, he was immediately made a minister – or if he ended up against the wall. That chap was a big fish; he must have been engaged in top-level politics. When I came back from interrogation, he said to me, 'How is it outside today – warm?'

For my turn to be interrogated had also come. But the way I was treated! First, I had to wait an hour in the corridor, then another in some empty room through which people crossed without paying me any particular attention. They were very preoccupied with something, or perhaps I was of no interest to them. After all, they had big-time political racketeers to deal with here, real crafty players, politicians and war criminals. Who was I?

I soon learnt pretty much what they took me for, or, to put it better – who they'd like to see me as. One particular functionary who finally took me for questioning – an intellectual actually, an old communist for sure – attempted to convince me that I had collaborated with the Gestapo, that I discriminated against Jews and that I had amassed a fortune through economic cooperation with the

Germans. I was convinced that he himself did not believe the accusations he was levelling, that he was doing it just in case, as investigative agencies the world over are wont to do. I admitted the change in nationality, but I categorically denied that I had done it for so-called base motives; I declared that my only reason for changing nationality was a desire to help the Poles. I am a weak person, my health is poor, my sight is feeble; I was unfit to take up arms in battle. So if I did have some contact with Germans, I used it not to harm, but to help the Poles. The man questioning me seemed tired, sleep-deprived; he rubbed his eyes with his fingers, leaned his head on his hand and seemed not to be listening too carefully to what I was saying – but now he livened up and began to observe me. He told me to tell him my life story.

I was prepared for this. I began with my childhood and finished with the moment of my arrest. I hid only two facts in my life: a short spell working with the editorial board of a certain aggressively nationalist paper which came out in Warsaw before the war. I counted on them not discovering that; it was essentially a brief episode. Someone informed my boss, an old-fashioned Piłsudski man; I was summoned to hear the following ultimatum from that vulgar legionary: 'Us or them. It's your choice . . .' I was vaguely interested in the movement that had formed around the publication, but not to the extent of risking my position; I broke off contact with the newspaper, having placed only two short articles with them. The other affair I kept silent about was obviously the business with my caretaker, or rather the first part of the story. The second part I alluded to in passing, in a way which could only bear witness to my modesty, and it seemed to incline the person sitting opposite favourably towards me. At the end of questioning, I found a way to ask if I could count on a defence counsel. My questioner was surprised that I should doubt it.

Two or three days later, I was transferred to a communal cell. I'd been demoted, clearly acknowledged to be a lower-calibre criminal. I should have rejoiced. But the atmosphere of that common cell quickly made life a misery. I found myself among people with whom I could not establish the slightest connection, let alone like them; I moved among them as though colliding against hard sharp objects which wounded my body.

The very first night, they cooked up a vulgar prank for me: a 'booting', a 'night interrogation', or whatever name that comedy goes by in prison jargon, which consists of being questioned by an alleged official detective. The day before, I'd overheard an abundance of tales, meant for me, about one such degenerate investigator who had a penchant for sexual themes and, with this in mind, would visit the prison by night; apparently he'd been in the neighbouring cell two nights in a row, so we could expect him here before too long. And indeed that very night I was woken from a deep sleep by the scraping of a key in the lock and the door creaking open. (These sounds, it later transpired, had been mimicked with the help of a bowl, a spoon and a stool.) I heard a voice ordering me, in a disgusting, eastern drawl, to get up and answer questions. I stood there in my underpants, shaking with cold and attempted to defend myself against accusations of robbing Poles, killing Jews, entering into liaisons with ageing German women, submitting to Nazi officers and raping children. Luckily, when the interrogator began to ask very detailed questions concerning my relations with women, someone couldn't keep it up and burst out laughing. The interrogation was over, but the merriment continued long and loud at my expense; the cell calmed down only when the guard began to harangue us as stupid baboons, disturbing the sleep of the rest.

So what types were doing time with me? My cellmates didn't hide their crimes: two were in for stealing sugar and shoe leather, meant for distribution among workers; one was in there – in his own words – over Jewish property; a third for some currency swindles; two for working for the local paper. Then there was an actor who'd played in the German theatre and a barber who took Gestapo clients. Our cell also briefly hosted two arrivals from the forest who believed that we should still be risking our necks – but against the Soviets now – and a fellow who was rumoured to be an old communist. Like it or not, I was compelled to listen to these conversations. All of them quite shamelessly spilt their guts for all they were worth against the government and socialism and badmouthed those who'd now come to power. My reticence to pronounce on the future of socialism created an atmosphere of suspicion; they took me for a snitch. Ridiculous people! I was further from socialism than any of them. I'd be ready to bet that those two barbarians from the forest, lice-ridden and unshaven, who were shooting at Soviet soldiers barely a week ago, were closer to socialism than I was. That old communist, too, would soon be making peace with his comrades. I would never be a socialist, but that's not important. My sympathies for those who win have nothing to do with conviction. I am above ideals; I don't give way to hesitation or confusion like all manner of idealists; I don't have the scruples of the patriots. I am above all that. Because I have no convictions.

*

I was interrogated a second time, which involved replying

to the same questions and repeating the same résumé. Then I returned once more to the communal cell and the days passed, one after another, waiting for the trial.

A few of us, including the barber who shaved the Gestapo, the two editors who'd collaborated with the Germans, and those who'd grown rich off the Jews, were now driven out to work by car. I never ran across that distinguished older gentleman with whom I'd shared a cell in the beginning, nor did I ever see the partisans or the former communist. They were clearly regarded as political prisoners and enjoyed some special rights. I was pleased not to have that distinction of dubious value conferred on me. As a rule, we were employed clearing the rubble from bombed-out houses or cleaning up roadways. I worked with my head down, I didn't look about, I didn't want to see anyone, nor did I wish to be seen. The work was light and no one hurried us; we moved like flies in spring. We could stock up on newspapers and cigarettes; some of us arranged to meet with family and friends.

But one day we were assigned a nasty job. We were driven beyond town by car, to where the entrenchments used to be. I know those parts, I used to go there as a student to study. In my day, the entrenchment slopes were densely covered in short grass, chamomile and thyme; an acacia grove blossomed white, wafting a stifling, soporific scent; it was peaceful, the bees hummed quietly. But now, where thyme once grew – the ground had been dug up. Mounds of yellow clay ran alongside deep trenches. People stood about pressing handkerchiefs to their faces. To one side, military personnel and civilians with armbands were officiating at a table strewn with papers and a typewriter. German prisoners were working in already excavated trenches; others were digging up the ground in new places. At the base of the trenches, in the mud, in the black slime, lay objects akin to the roots of trees as one might see them tossed on to riverbanks after a flood. More objects, some bound together with wire, lay alongside, on the grass. We were given rubber boots and gloves and ordered to climb into the trenches and help the Germans. A tall, thin German prisoner wearing glasses was leaning against the side of a trench and vomiting.

Seized with a livid fury, I yelled at him in German, 'You swine, why didn't you throw up when you were shooting at them!' But a moment later I too was vomiting; well, we all were, one after another.

Returning to prison in the car that afternoon, I felt very ill. I thought, for the first time, that only a crime that's been publicly exposed deserves to be labelled a true crime. A person who has committed a crime must hear from others that he is a criminal, because the conscience . . . but let's not speak of the conscience. I don't think I have ever felt so lousy in my life. I had visions of endless lines of people in striped clothing, photos of gas chambers, piles of corpses lying on the ground and rows of corpses hanging from gallows – everything the newspapers were teeming with now. Yes, I felt very bad. My one comfort was a thought that finally came to mind – that all those many bodies rotting there, in the ditches, did not include mine . . . I returned to the prison with relief; you could say that I was even happy somehow when they finally closed the iron gates behind me. Our dark, dirty, latrine-smelling cell seemed bright and clean to me, and the companions to whom I returned sympathetic. I learnt that in my absence a lawyer had been and asked about me – about other prisoners too in fact. They predicted a swift trial.

Two days later, the lawyer arrived. He was a small, bald, sweaty man. Hastening in, he gave the impression that he was handling all the business in town at a run. He told me he'd read my bill of indictment, that I too would receive it shortly, and he asked for the names and addresses of witnesses. I gave four people: my vacation landlady whom I'd helped to hide the rifle; my caretaker and his wife; and – with some hesitation – Zofia. The small, perspiring little man wrote everything down in a thick, shabby notebook and rushed on elsewhere. I gave Zofia's name because I hadn't counted on her being found. But perhaps eight or ten days later, I was summoned to the visiting room where my sweaty, busy lawyer was waiting for me.

'My dear sir,' he greeted me, wiping his brow with a handkerchief, 'you were born under a lucky star! Do you know who citizen Zofia is?! You don't? You guess, but you're not sure? Then you'll soon find out. And that mountain woman! And your caretaker? Why so modest, I ask you?' He leaned closer, so that the supervisor wouldn't hear, 'Not only will you get out, you'll get a medal . . .'

*

I saw the prison barber, went for a bath, cleaned my shoes, beat and brushed my clothes. I performed all these activities in a kind of trance; I was compliant, calm and impassive. At one point, I was struck by the amusing thought that in such a mental state and thus prepared, shaved, washed and combed, I could just as well stand against the wall. I jest, of course, but there's something in it. I was perfectly aware – based on conversations with fellow prisoners and from what my lawyer muttered to me in monosyllables – that I could expect two years in prison at worst. Whatever lay ahead for me, it was better than what I'd experienced.

So I sat in the dock accompanied by the policeman who'd escorted me. On the wall above the empty judges'

table, which was tightly upholstered in green baize, hung
a white eagle against a red background. It was the first
case of the day: the chamber filled slowly with people, no
doubt regular attendees of trials. They studied my face as
though they expected to guess at the crime that weighed
on my conscience and the outrages that I'd prepared for
the public. I turned away and looked through the misted
windowpanes at the roofs of the houses and trees already
budding green. I didn't think about anything; I carried
on counting the chimneys, the little garret windows and
the pigeons perched on gutters until the moment I heard,
'All rise for the court!' The wheels were set in motion.
The chairman of the judges read the bill of indictment
so indistinctly that had I been unfamiliar with its con-
tents, I would not have understood a single word, after
which he asked me if I was pleading guilty. I replied that I
was not. My declaration made no impression, no one was
surprised. The judges, prosecution and defence did not
deign even to glance at the person who had failed to plead
guilty. The wheels continued to turn. While I was recount-
ing my story, the judges leafed through documents, the
defence sat leaning his head on his hand, and the prosecution picked his nose furtively. The chairman wished to
hear from me regarding my past, including, among other
things, why I had been exempted from military service,
where I had worked just before the war, how I had come
to acquire a position in a German office and how much I
earned there. Neither the defence nor the prosecution had
any questions for me. I sat down. The chairman called on
the defence to open and summoned the first witness. The
office porter entered the chamber. He was dressed in a
uniform issued back in German times, but with the stripes
unpicked from the sleeves, and he held a new, brown-and-
white checked cap in his hand.

In answer to the question did he recognize the accused, he responded without looking at me, 'Yes . . .'

'Does the witness know that the accused was a so-called *Volksdeutscher*?'

'Yes.'

'How does the witness know?'

'Everyone in the office knew.'

'If I may,' the prosecutor spoke up. The porter turned his head warily. He was a witness for the prosecution.

'As a porter, the witness must have had occasion to see the documents of the accused, an identity card or papers?'

'No, I didn't.'

'But the accused must sometimes have given the witness his ration card, for the witness to collect some part of it? It was a common practice.'

The porter pricked up his ears, for the subject of food ration cards was not a pleasant one for him; after all, he'd done good business with them, trading in vodka, saccharine and lemons. In exchange, he'd supplied the Germans with sausage, eggs and honey from the countryside.

'Sometimes, maybe once or twice . . .'

'So what kind of cards were they – Polish or German?'

'They were German, I mean, ones for Germans . . .'

'And what sort of cards did the witness have?'

'Who, me?'

'Yes.'

'Well, Polish ones, for Poles.'

'And which cards had the bigger rations? The Polish or the German?'

'The German ones, obviously!' the porter said cheerfully.

'So why didn't you sign up as a German, to get better rations?'

At this point, the lawyer propping his head up showed

himself a being of exceptional vigilance; he jumped up
suddenly and said, 'Your Honour, may I permit myself to
point out that this question . . .'

'The prosecution's question is overruled,' said the
chairman, and the prosecutor bowed and said 'thank
you', but the porter didn't understand this exchange –
and effused with gusto, 'I, Your Honour, couldn't become
a *Volksdeutscher* because I didn't know a single word of
German. It wasn't until I was in the office that I learnt
a few words: *danke, bitte, jawohl* . . .' Laughter rippled
through the chamber, and the porter added, 'Besides, I
was a Pole . . .'

'Quiet, please. I thank the witness. The witness is free
to go.' The porter bowed and returned to the bench. The
next to give evidence was the office messenger boy. He
confirmed that I was a *Volksdeutscher*, and said I spoke
German with the Germans, and Polish with him and the
porter. He hadn't noticed my being on particularly intimate terms with the Germans. In answer to the prosecutor's
question, did I use the greeting '*Heil Hitler*', he replied in
the affirmative. When the prosecutor asked if the witness
knew of any instances of ill-treatment of Poles on the part
of the accused – he replied in the negative, but then cor-
rected himself and said he might not have noticed as he
was seldom in the office, since his business was conducted
at various bureaus and at the post office, or he simply
'skived off' and went to underground youth meetings or
distributed news-sheets and leaflets. He was asked further
what he did in the office and what sort of tasks fell to him.

The messenger was an intelligent boy, but when he
started to work for us, he was still too wet behind the
ears to know what was going on. And this was meant to
be a witness for the prosecution! The case dragged on, my
guilt began to die a natural death. So far, the witnesses

for the prosecution had not harmed me unduly; now if the witnesses for the defence could help just a little.

At last my landlady, from whom I'd rented a room during the summer vacation, was summoned from the corridor. She came in and stood before the judge, not one bit changed from the time when I'd stayed there. She was neatly dressed, wearing a new headscarf. She answered in a quiet voice, adjusting the knot under her chin from time to time, or pulling the scarf forward over her forehead.

'So, what's the story with this rifle?'

'Well, Your Honour, my husband happened to be away, because he'd gone to the sawmill for wood. And in the night my son returned from war, with that very rifle.'

'And what happened next with the rifle?'

'We hid it.'

'Who hid it?'

My landlady turned round, glanced at me, adjusted her headscarf and said, 'We hid it together.'

'You mean the accused helped the witness to hide the rifle, yes?'

'That's right.'

'And what happened to the rifle?'

'Nothing. It stayed there.'

'That is, the Germans didn't find it?'

'Good God, no . . .'

'Are there any questions?'

My small, bald lawyer jumped from the bench like a jack-in-the-box. He pushed up his sleeves and, wrapping himself in his oversized black gown, declared: 'If it please the witness. Did the accused know precisely where the rifle had been hidden?'

'Well yes, in the outhouse. He shone the torch for me.'

'And what happened to the rifle later?'

'It stayed put. And later on my son took it to the forest.'

'That is to say, to the partisans?'

'Yes, the partisans.'

'Thank you,' my lawyer swept a triumphant gaze over the judges and prosecution.

'Are there any more questions?'

The prosecutor shrugged, then turned his head and observed me for a moment.

My landlady tightened the knot under her chin and went to sit on the bench. Her husband was waiting for her with a young man in a grey jacket whom I recognized, not without difficulty, as her son. The chairman was rifling through some papers attached to the bill of indictment and whispering to his colleagues. Silence reigned; I felt the warm friendly eyes of the public upon me.

A moment later, the next witness entered the chamber, the tenement caretaker. He was dressed in his Sunday best, a black suit with jutting shoulders, a brown, ex-German shirt and a red tie. He strode in assertively, like a man who knew what job he was here to do. The questions were repeated of whether the witness was related to the accused, followed by the same cautionary ritual bidding of the witness to speak the truth – and my key witness spoke.

'Apparently, the accused helped the witness when the witness was arrested by the Germans?' the chairman asked.

'That's right, Your Honour.'

'Please recount what happened.'

'I was arrested on 7 December 1941 on the charge that I was a Pole, that I was raising my children in a patriotic spirit, and that I possessed forbidden books which were, in fact, found at my home.'

'And what were these books?'

'*The Knights of the Cross* and a school textbook, *The*

History of Poland, along with some leaflets. When the accused found out what had happened to me, he came to my wife and said he would try to do something to get me out of prison. And, in fact, a week later, I was freed . . .' My caretaker stopped at this point, looked at the prosecutor and then at the lawyer and added, 'I just want to mention, Your Honour, that had I stayed in prison, I would have faced the same threat as all Poles: death or the camps . . .'

There was a moment's hush. The chairman asked, 'Are there any questions?'

The lawyer responded, 'Perhaps the witness can tell the judge whether the assistance granted the witness by the accused was disinterested, or if the accused demanded some kind of compensation?'

'The accused refused any money. When my wife mentioned it, he said he was doing it only for the children. Then, when I left prison, I headed to the accused's place to thank him. And, sir . . . Well, I took something to drink with me, a bite to chase it down, but we drank only one glass apiece and the accused told me to take the rest home, to my wife and children.'

'I thank the witness,' said the lawyer.

'Will there be any questions?' asked the chairman. 'The witness is free to step down.'

I watched the caretaker as he stepped briskly towards the bench and only then did I notice the two lads sitting there. They were very alike, with the same haircut, pale faces and thin necks. They were staring at me; I smiled at them. The chairman called on the caretaker's wife, but she was in hospital following an operation, and the lawyer drew the judges' attention to the written declaration attached. The judge wet his finger and leafed through the dossier. He removed a small green slip and placed it before him on the table. Again, it fell silent. I turned my head and looked out of the window. I thought how I couldn't actually really remember how it had been with the caretaker. At that moment, I was convinced that I'd saved him. Wasn't that the case? If no one but me and that German, who might be rotting somewhere near Stalingrad, since he'd been sent to the eastern front – if no one else knew the truth – then why couldn't I believe what I found it convenient and congenial to believe?

Suddenly, I heard Zofia's surname – and I saw her. She came in with quick resolute steps and stopped in front of the grating. In the crook of her left arm hung a beautiful little bag, like a bomboniere; she leaned her right hand, clad in a thin white glove, on the baluster. She seemed to me a long way from where I was sitting, although in reality I don't know if it can have been more than ten paces. I heard her singsong borderland accent. This usually silent woman, of whom I'd always known so little, was now saying that during the Occupation she'd worked for Polish military intelligence, in the section countering the so-called *Vergeltungswaffen*: remote guided missiles, in other words. Thanks to our acquaintance of many years, originating from the time of my friendship with her husband, she could trust me and enlist me into collaboration. I was one of those who had done great service for the cause. I had made my flat available, stored documents and conspiratorial material, provided information and supplied the organization with German company notepaper. Zofia recounted all this in a quiet voice, so that I had to prick up my ears to hear. I watched her slight, graceful figure; she was wearing a new, beautifully cut suit, her legs in stockings so fine they were barely visible. She would raise her small, white-gloved hand occasionally, make some gesture in the air, then calmly rest it again on the wooden balustrade. I listened to what she said, and at moments I would lose my sense of reality; I stopped believing in what had been; it seemed to me completely improbable that I had ever slept with this woman.

*

I returned home in the evening, in a droshky with the hood lowered. I didn't want to be seen by anyone; I was wearing clothes crumpled after disinfection, without a tie, and was already in need of a shave since the morning. I scaled the stairs slowly, leaning on the banister. Prison had not favoured my health; I felt weakened, my heart beat hard, something pressed tight in my chest. It was quiet in the stairwell, just the distant cries of children from some neighbouring courtyard, the barking of dogs and the echo of a ball being kicked. I had survived this whole vileness, then; I was alive, free, I'd returned to my own flat! Here I was, at the very door. The Germans had lost the war, but I had not. If my health permitted, I still had whole long years of life ahead. Electricity and gas bill reminders had piled up in my postbox, with some questionnaires and a summons to the council. The varnish on my door was flaking in several places; the brass plate and spyhole were tarnished. I turned the key in the lock and met the familiar smell of home, preserved undisturbed over many months. Here was my room, just as I'd left it on the day of my arrest – the same furniture, the same thick Żywiec carpet, pictures and books. The bicycle leaned against the wall in the hallway. I hadn't lost any of these objects, nothing had been taken from me, I hadn't been burgled while away in prison. The building which housed my flat had not been bombed or burnt down. I had returned to my things which were waiting for me, merely grown a little older, perhaps. Everything was covered in a thick layer of dust, the windows were misted over. I had much work ahead to restore order to my room, to make it clean and habitable again. I opened the window; the evening chill blew in from the street. The sun was setting, but it couldn't be seen; it just cast its red reflection against the windowpanes of the building opposite. Red and white obituaries had been pasted on the tenement gates, probably for the three young people who'd been arrested by the Germans back at the beginning of the occupation. I'd seen masses of such obituaries all over town, in gateways, on fences, on the walls of churches. The tenement opposite mine stood black and empty, as though deserted. But on the second-floor balcony – yes! – it was her, that same, immortal, indestructible old lady whom I'd known by sight for many years. She sat in her wicker chair, her legs wrapped in a blanket. Her little shrivelled face, leaning towards one shoulder, was facing in my direction; but the little old lady surely couldn't see me.

I pottered about the house aimlessly for a while; it was too late today to begin tidying up. In any case, I didn't feel especially good. I took off my clothes and Lysol-stinking underwear and went to the bathroom. While the bath filled with water, I had a chance to examine my body in the mirror. I hadn't done that in a long while, and now was a most appropriate moment – I'd succeeded in extracting my delicate, fragile human existence intact from these ghastly times. It had to be admitted that I hadn't come out of it too badly: I hadn't paid too high a price for the one valuable thing that exists in this world – my own life.

My body was very much wasted after winter and the prison. My muscles had grown flabby; my skin was pale and unhealthy, sprinkled with blemishes and pimples here and there. In a few places, I discovered growths which

I'd never seen before on my body: bruises, tiny winding veins. My legs were very wretched: sharp knees and emaciated thighs. The sight of my toes moved and saddened me – they were so pitiful, crooked, shrunken. I had never boasted an exceptionally masculine build, and had always been slightly prone to putting on weight; now, after prison soup and groats, I'd developed quite a protruding stomach, and gained flesh on my buttocks.

I examined my face up close; unfortunately, my hair, eyebrows and the stubble on my cheeks revealed greying growth. My wrinkles had multiplied. I found two new warts near my nose and on my forehead. Back in the day, in my early youth, before I'd become a cautious person even in my dreams – I'd often imagine myself a hero. I'd pull faces in the mirror, wrinkle my brow, make a furrow above my nose with my fingers, which, I was convinced, was a mark of vigour and determination. I'd pout, attempting to give my lips an expression of strength, pride, disdain for life. Equipped with such qualities, I could, at the age of ten or twelve, be the defender of the weak and persecuted, a freedom fighter, a man ready to sacrifice money or even his life for his ideals. It's amusing that in the country where I live, so many people retain these infantile delusions to the end of their lives! But there's no shortage of such crackpots everywhere.

It's not pleasant to ascertain signs of ageing in oneself. I was nearing forty; my body already bore clear traces of wear and tear. How little time there was left before my existence succumbed to complete devastation – barely twenty, maybe twenty-five years. That's the average age a man attains in the part of Europe where I live. And to think that someone might have the right to demand that I willingly agree to live a considerably shorter time! By what right? In the name of what?

Bathing stimulates the imagination considerably. Sitting in the bath, all manner of ideas came to mind regarding my future. One way or another, life would pan out – I was sure of one thing: I was going to work sincerely and without reservation, because that is my attitude. Victors are strong and fine – for as long as they retain their position, of course. If, one fine day, they come a cropper – so much the worse for them. But let's abandon that dangerous thought; there's no sign of that happening in my lifetime. For now I'd survived, I was alive, I was free; *basta*.

My bath refreshed me and really lifted my mood. I was close to feeling like someone completely satisfied with life. I say close – since I didn't feel absolutely happy. Somehow, something was bothering me, some trifling glitch, as though a tiny pebble had fallen into my shoe. I climbed out of the bath, pulled out the plug and rubbed myself with a fresh scented towel while the dirty water drained away. Then I set about tidying my toenails. I pondered meanwhile, just what could be hindering my sense of being an absolutely happy person? Perhaps, deep inside, I harboured some hidden grudge against people and the world that I hadn't been forced, as is often the case in wartime, into some act of heroism against my will? Perhaps a life which emerges intact from such an adventure later holds some unusual, special value for a person?

Such were the thoughts that finally crossed my mind; well, everyone has moments of weakness . . ."